MW00575677

To Dominic

Text copyright © Vyanne Samuels 1988   Illustrations copyright © Jennifer Northway 1988
All rights reserved. No part of this book may be reproduced or transmitted in any form
or by any means, electronic or mechanical, including photocopying, recording, or by any
information storage and retrieval system, without permission in writing from the Publisher.
Four Winds Press, Macmillan Publishing Company, 866 Third Avenue, New York, NY 10022
First published 1988 in Great Britain by The Bodley Head Ltd
First American Edition 1989
Printed in the United States of America

10 9 8 7 6 5 4 3 2 1

Library of Congress Cataloging-in-Publication Data
Samuels, Vyanne.   Carry go bring come.
Summary: A young boy has his hands full when he helps his sister prepare for
her wedding. [1. Weddings—Fiction.] I. Northway, Jennifer, date, ill. II. Title.
PZ7.S1945Car 1989 [E] 89-1528
ISBN 0-02-778121-6

Carry Go
Bring Come

Vyanne Samuels

Illustrated by Jennifer Northway

Four Winds Press
New York

It was Saturday morning at Leon's house. It was a
big Saturday morning at Leon's house. It was
Marcia's wedding day. Marcia was Leon's sister.

Everyone in the house was getting ready for the big Saturday morning. Everyone was getting ready for the big wedding.

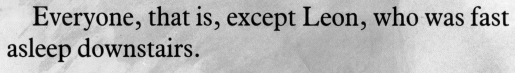

Everyone, that is, except Leon, who was fast
asleep downstairs.

"Wake up, Leon!" shouted his mother upstairs.
But Leon did not move.
"Wake up, Leon!" shouted his sister Marlene
upstairs.
But Leon did not move.

Leon's mother and his sisters, Marlene and Marcia, were so busy taking big blue rollers out of their hair that they forgot to shout at Leon to wake up again.

They were getting ready for the big day.
They were getting ready for Marcia's wedding.

"Wake up, Leon," said Grandma softly downstairs.

Leon's two eyes opened up immediately.
Leon was awake.

"Carry this up to your mother," said Grandma, handing him a pink silk flower.

Leon ran upstairs to the bedroom with the pink silk flower. But before he could knock on the door, his sister Marcia called to him.

"Wait a little," she said, and she handed him a white veil. "Carry this down to Grandma."

So Leon put the flower between his teeth and the veil in his two hands and ran down the stairs to Grandma.

When he got to his grandma's door, she called
to him before he could knock.
"Wait a little," she said. He waited.

"Carry these up to Marlene," she said, and she poked a pair of blue shoes out at him.

So Leon put the veil on his head, kept
the flower between his teeth, and carried the shoes
in his two hands.

He tripped upstairs to Marlene.

But when he got to the bedroom door, Marlene called to him before he could knock.

"Wait a little," she said, and she poked a pair of yellow gloves through the door. "Carry these down to Grandma."

So Leon put the gloves on his hands,

the shoes on his feet,

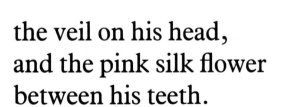

the veil on his head,
and the pink silk flower
between his teeth.

He wobbled downstairs to Grandma, who called to him before he could knock.

"Wait a little," she said. He waited.

"Carry this to Marcia," she said, and she poked a green bottle of perfume through the door.

"Mind how you go," she said.

So Leon climbed the stairs carefully holding the green bottle of perfume, carefully wearing the yellow gloves, carefully dragging the blue shoes, carefully balancing the white veil, carefully biting the pink silk flower . . . when suddenly he could go no further and shouted

"HELP!" from the middle of the stairs.

He nearly swallowed the flower.

His mother ran out of the room upstairs,
his sister Marlene ran out of the room upstairs,

and Grandma rushed out of her room downstairs.

There was a big silence. They all looked at Leon.

"Look 'pon his feet!" said his mother.

"Look 'pon his fingers and his hands!" said Marlene.

"Look 'pon his head!" said Grandma.

"Look 'pon his mouth!" said Marcia.

And they all let go a big laugh!

Leon looked like a bride!

One by one, Mother, Marcia, Marlene, and
Grandma took away the pink silk flower, the white
veil, the green bottle of perfume, the blue
shoes, and the yellow gloves.

"When am I going to get dressed for the wedding?" asked Leon, wearing just his pajamas now.

"Just wait a little!" said Grandma.

Leon's two eyes opened wide.
"YOU MEAN I HAVE TO WAIT A
LITTLE?" he shrieked.

And before anyone could answer, he ran
downstairs...

and jumped straight back into his bed, without

waiting even a little.

DATE DUE

FEB. 02			
MAR 2 9			

HIGHSMITH   #LO-45102